THE CHIMNEY WITCHES

Victoria Whitehead

Illustrated by Linda North

ORCHARD BOOKS   *New York & London*

A DIVISION OF FRANKLIN WATTS, INC.

ORCHARD BOOKS

387 Park Avenue South
New York, NY 10016
20 Torbay Road
Markham, Ontario 23P 1G6
Divisions of Franklin Watts, Inc.

MANUFACTURED IN THE UNITED STATES OF AMERICA

Book design by Tere Lo Prete

10   9   8   7   6   5   4   3   2
Text of this book is set in 12 Monticello

Library of Congress Cataloging-in-Publication Data
Whitehead, Victoria.
    The chimney witches.
    Summary: When eight-year-old Ellen meets the witches living in the chimney of her house, she experiences the most exciting Halloween of her life.
    [1. Witches—Fiction.   2. Halloween—Fiction]
I. Title.
PZ7.W5858Ch   1987   [Fic]   87-5731
ISBN 0-531-05707-0
ISBN 0-531-08307-1 (lib. bdg.)

Contents

THE CHIMNEY WITCHES

I

The Witch in the Chimney

*E*llen felt herself drifting into sleep in the armchair. She had just excused herself from the dinner table. The rest of the family were still eating. Toby, who was only just three, had lost some of his peas on the floor and was protesting in his high chair. Mom looked at Ellen anxiously.

"She's not well, you know," she said to Dad.

"Wake up, Ellen," said Dad, "or you'll never sleep tonight."

Ellen opened her eyes and said mysteriously, "Oh, I never sleep at night."

Richard snickered, but Dad said, "Why ever not?"

"Too much noise," said Ellen.

"Too much noise *all* night?" said Dad. "It must be the traffic outside."

"No. Not ordinary noises," said Ellen. "Funny noises, from the fireplace. They keep me awake."

"But you've never mentioned them before," said Mom. "And the fireplace has been bricked up for years. What do you mean, funny noises?"

"Well, actually," said Ellen, glaring at Richard, who was treating it all as a joke, "there's a witch living in the chimney."

Mom picked up some of Toby's lost peas and Richard laughed out loud. He was eleven and had long outgrown such fantasies.

"A witch in the chimney? How do you know?"

"I just know," muttered Ellen.

"Well, with Halloween tomorrow and a witch living by your bed, you'd just better watch out that you don't get changed into a slimy green frog in the night," said Richard. "I'm not kissing you to change you back into a girl again. I'd rather keep you in a pond in the garden and feed you a fly occasionally."

"Richard, for goodness sake go up and do your homework," said Mom crossly. "And leave her alone. Can't you see she's not well? Stop teasing."

"Sorry, El." Richard grinned. "All right, I will kiss you if I absolutely have to, but not unless I absolutely have to."

"Richard! Homework!" said Dad in his loud homework voice. And Richard went upstairs.

Mom lifted Toby down from his chair and Ellen smiled behind her hand. She didn't mind being teased. She was used to it. Richard, who was three years older than she was, had been teasing her all her life and she still loved him. Being teased was much better than being ignored.

Sometime later, Ellen put on her nightgown and brushed her teeth. She settled down in front of the television while Mom put Toby to bed. She was looking forward to going to bed herself, but she knew there was no point in going too early. The mysterious happenings in the chimney would not begin for a while.

Richard was doing his homework in his bedroom. Next day he was to take a music exam and, if he passed, the family had decided that he could go and stay with his grandma, who lived near a special school where he could take advanced music classes. Ellen did not want him to pass that exam. Other people's brothers didn't have to go to schools twenty miles away from home and she didn't want him to go either.

"Come along, Ellen," said Mom when she had finished with Toby. "Up you go to bed. You look as if you need a good night's sleep." The program Ellen had been watching wasn't finished but, for once, she decided not to make a fuss. She had a feeling that the mystery of the witch in the chimney was going to unfold for her tonight. It was the night before Halloween and anything might happen!

She ran upstairs.

"Are you sure you want to sleep in your own room to-night?" asked Mom, following her. Ellen switched on her bedroom light and looked around her bright yellow walls hung with posters. The old fireplace was painted white and there were books and ornaments on the mantelpiece.

"Yes, I'm sure," she replied. "I don't know if she's a bad witch or not, but I'm not at all scared."

Mom shook her head.

"Hop into bed," she said. "Witches in chimneys indeed! Whatever next?" Then she left hurriedly because Toby was shouting that the cover had fallen off his bed and that he was cold.

Richard opened his bedroom door and called, "Goodnight, El. Watch out for witches. Croak. Croak. Croak!"

"Goodnight, you big fat toad!" called Ellen. "Goodnight!" and she pulled the knotted string that swung above her bed and switched off the light. Tonight the darkness felt very dark indeed.

Ellen heard Mom say goodnight five times to Toby because he kept calling her back for something or other. Then she and Dad watched television and Richard began to get ready for bed. Ellen's bedroom door was open and the landing light threw the shape of a number one across the darkness of the room. It stretched across to the fireplace and Ellen's eyes followed it to the mantelpiece, where they alighted on a gold painted box with brightly colored symbols on the lid. Ellen had no idea how the box came to be there. It had just appeared that very morning. Inside it, on a bed of red velvet, she had found a long gold chain encircling a beautiful medallion. Engraved there was the picture of a pointed hat, maybe the hat of a witch or a wizard. Around the edge were written the words *Medallion of Middle Magic*.

Ellen's gaze wandered from the box to the gap in the curtains, through which she could see the sky—no stars or moon, just swirling clouds. She closed her eyes and fell asleep.

It was some time later, when everything was quiet in the rest of the house, that the noises in Ellen's fireplace began. There was a bang and a few thumps and the sound of a voice, humming a familiar song. Ellen's eyes were now wide open again as she lay in bed and wondered exactly what was going on. There *was* a witch in the chimney. She knew that for sure. The family did not believe in it, but she would show them. She was going to show them all.

2

Rufus

The witch in the chimney was called Weird Hannah and she had just gotten out of bed. She had recently left her country cottage to settle down in town and, as soon as she had seen the chimney of Ellen's fireplace, she had known it would be the ideal place to live. It had not taken her long to make the chimney parlor cozy. She had moved in with a huge black cat, several small white mice and a naughty witch boy son whose name was Rufus. Hannah often swore that one day Rufus would worry her to a shadow.

Today was to be a busy day. With Halloween coming

there was a lot to do. Hannah was preparing a caldron of oatmeal and Rufus was still in bed.

"Time to get up, Rufus!" cried Hannah, poking him with a skinny witch finger.

"Not getting up," mumbled Rufus from beneath a bedspread sewn with stars.

"It'll be time for Night Witchery classes," said his mother, "just as soon as you've finished this lovely oatmeal," and she hummed a few bars of the National Anthem, which generally meant she was in a fairly good mood.

"Don't want any oatmeal. Not going to Night Witchery classes," muttered Rufus into his pillow.

"Come along, Rufus. Mother's waiting," said Hannah impatiently, and she hit his bed with a ladle. Rufus sat up in surprise. He yawned a yawn like a ship's horn and rolled slowly out of bed. He was a skinny boy in striped pajamas and his hair stuck out like the spikes on a porcupine.

Hannah took him by the ear, sat him down at the table and ladled a dollop of oatmeal into a bowl.

"Don't want any oatmeal," said Rufus.

"Eat," said his mother fiercely.

Rufus picked up his bowl and dropped it upside down

on the floor. The oatmeal oozed everywhere. The cat decided it was safer under the bed, and the white mice ran into the breadbox. Hannah's good mood had completely vanished. She was extremely angry, and let out a long screech.

"You stupid boy!" she cried.

So far this had been a normal morning in the chimney parlor. It was no wonder that Ellen heard so many peculiar noises.

Halloween was only a day away, and Hannah had a lot of spells to practice, so she was feeling extra edgy. This made her extra cross with Rufus, and Rufus was becoming extra naughty.

"By the Great Wizard of Ages Ago, you're a bad boy, Rufus! I swear I'll put a spell on you one of these days!"

"I can use spells too, you know, mother," retorted Rufus and he stuck out his tongue.

"You're too young to use them properly," snapped Hannah.

"I can use spells! I can! I can!" cried Rufus, eyes blazing, and he stamped his foot with rage.

Hannah grabbed her wand, which she kept by the breadbox, and the mice ran under the bed. The cat leapt onto the highest shelf it could find and knocked a plate onto the floor, where it smashed to pieces. Hannah waved her wand threateningly. It crackled and spat like water in hot fat.

"Now just get yourself ready for Night Witchery classes before I turn you into a frog!" she ordered. Then, calming down a little, she shook her head, scratched it with her wand and sighed deeply.

"Go to your classes, then you *will* be able to use spells like me and Uncle Whizoon," she pleaded. "Be a good boy, Rufus, or you'll worry me to a shadow."

But this morning, Rufus didn't feel like being a good boy. This Halloween, he was going to show them that, when it came to spells, he was a man.

"I'll show you I can use spells," he said. "I'm going to win a Medallion this year. I've been practicing. I'll show you. I'll show you." And he ran to the chest where the spell ingredients were kept.

"Don't be so silly, Rufus," said Hannah. "Spells are dangerous. You know spells are dangerous."

But Rufus was already going through the carefully labelled boxes and emptying their contents onto the floor. There was a handful of flour, a spoonful of soot, a box of worms, a jar of fog—he was now throwing things wildly about the room.

"I'll show you! I'll show Uncle Whizoon!" cried Rufus as the ingredients began to spark and crackle.

Bat's wings, sawdust, baking powder, Stilton cheese . . . just like machine gun fire, the spells were shooting out in all directions, spattering the walls and lighting up the room in different colors.

"You see," sang Rufus. "Spells. Fantastic spells."

The cat and mice were changing shape and color rapidly and Hannah was growing fatter and thinner by the minute.

"Stop! Stop!" she cried. "Do you want to kill us all?"

The commotion had now become so loud that Ellen jumped out of bed and ran to the wall. There were poppings and fizzings and thumpings and bumpings and screechings and howlings. If it was like this tonight, what would it be like on Halloween? she thought. She banged on the wall with her fist, but it was clear that nobody could hear.

Rufus was now scared half to death and had run back to bed and buried himself under the cover. As for Weird Hannah, she had stopped growing fatter and thinner, and was steadily blowing up like a balloon. The furniture in the parlor began to fall over, and pots and pans began to dance with life. Just as things were coming to a climax, a jar of ketchup fell to the floor and smashed. The ketchup mixed with the mess on the floor. There were a few quiet moments, like a gathering of forces before a sneeze, then a giant explosion!

Ellen fell over backwards.

"What in the world can be happening?" she gasped, as she rubbed herself where it hurt and struggled to her feet. Then she looked carefully at her hands to make sure that she had not been changed into a frog. It was hard to tell in the dark, but her fingers still seemed to be fairly pink.

"Thank goodness," she said to herself.

Now there was such a long silence that she just had to go back to the fireplace and call through the wall.

"Is everything all right?"

"What a stupid question!" came a muffled reply. "Of course it isn't!"

"What's the matter?" called Ellen.

"Help! Help!" cried Rufus.

"What can I do?" asked Ellen.

"Up on the roof!" Rufus shouted.

"Up on the roof? How am I supposed to get up on the roof?" gasped Ellen.

"You can! You can!" said Rufus.

"How?"

A terrible wailing sound began and seemed to rise up be-hind the wall and settle somewhere above.

"What was that?" shouted Ellen.

"My mother," said Rufus. "She's stuck in the chimney. Listen while I give you a spell."

"A spell?" said Ellen. Now something really was going to happen. It would certainly give Richard a shock if she did change into a frog, after all his laughing and teasing. Rufus was busily looking around for the right spell and Hannah's wailing at the top of the chimney sounded like a police car siren.

At last Rufus yelled, "Right. Are you ready?"

"I'm ready!" cried Ellen.

"Then listen!" said Rufus.

> *"Moan and grizzle*
> *Stamp and twizzle*
> *Three times round*
> *Now off the ground.*

All right?"

Ellen looked about her in bewilderment.

"What must I do?" she said.

"Say the spell!" cried Rufus. "Follow the instructions. But hurry!"

She was quite good at learning poems, but Ellen was in such a state of excitement that she found it hard to concentrate. She breathed in deeply, and began as loudly as she could.

> *"Moan and grizzle*
> *Bump and twizzle . . . ."*

"No! No! Stamp!" bawled Rufus.

"Sorry," called Ellen.

"*Stamp*, not bump. *Stamp. Stamp and twizzle.*"

"Oh, yes," said Ellen, then she cleared her throat and began again.

> *"Moan and grizzle*
> *Stamp and twizzle*
> *Three . . . .*

Three? Did you say three?"

"Yes. Yes," cried Rufus. "Three."

"Moan and grizzle
Stamp and twizzle
Three times round
Now off the ground."

Ellen raced through the rhyme as quickly as she could. She stamped and she twizzled until she was dizzy. As she did so she heard some even stranger noises than before. A ringing and a buzzing, and the sound of water running down a plug hole. A roaring, sucking, spinning sound. The room spun around her then parts of it seemed to peel away leaving patches of blackness like old paint on a half-stripped wall. Eventually, the whole room had spun away and she was left in darkness. It was the spookiest thing that had ever happened to her, and yet she felt strangely calm.

Above her a tiddlywink of a moon slid from behind a cloud, and she saw that she was standing on a roof, with tiles shining beneath her feet. She was looking up at a chimney, towering black against the sky, and, in the moonlight, she saw a very strange sight indeed.

Poking out of the chimney pot there was a furious face, topped by a tall black hat which was slightly askew.

The face was, of course, Weird Hannah's, but to Ellen it was the cross and peculiar face that had been sneaking into her dreams for so long. She didn't know whether to laugh or scream. Weird Hannah did not give her time to do either. She was not going to put up with any shilly-shallying around. She had stopped wailing and was glowering as if Ellen had done something terrible.

"I'm stuck," she said accusingly. "Help me."

"I'm sorry," said Ellen politely. "What would you like me to do?"

"That wicked boy messed up my spells and turned me fat like a balloon. I've sailed up here and now I'm stuck. He doesn't know how to change me back either, so I shall be up here for ever. Who will make his oatmeal? Who will send him to school?"

She moaned a long moan then looked fiercely at Ellen.

"Don't just stand there," she snapped. "Do something."

"What shall I do?" asked Ellen again.

"Push!" Hannah said.

Ellen climbed carefully up the roof to the chimney and removed Hannah's hat. She put it down beside her, then she placed both hands on the top of the witch's head.

"Pull, boy, pull!" yelled Hannah to Rufus below. And the

joint operation began. Ellen pushed and pushed and Rufus pulled and pulled.

"Harder! Harder!" cried Hannah.

Ellen pushed harder until she felt a slight movement beneath her hands. Slowly at first, Hannah moved downwards, then all of a sudden, like a cork popping out of, or in this case into, a bottle, she popped inside the chimney pot and disappeared into the darkness below.

"You've forgotten your hat," Ellen called down the chimney. She could hear the echo of her own voice but there was no reply. She picked up the hat from beside her and leaned over for a better look, but she completely lost her balance and fell headlong into the chimney.

3
The Witch's Parlor

*E*llen tumbled around and around, down and down the chimney, and after a long dark fall, she found herself flat on her back in a little candle-lit room below, still clutching the witch's hat in both hands. Unfortunately, she had fallen on top of the witch, who was a bit squashed. But Weird Hannah was, for the moment, the shape of a beach ball, so she soon filled out again and struggled to her feet. She wasn't very pleased, however.

Ellen stood up, too, and looked around the parlor. What a state it was in! There were six green mice eating the remains of some Stilton cheese and a black cat with purple stripes was staring down from a high shelf. Rufus was sitting on a heap of pots and pans, and the table was upside down on the bed.

Weird Hannah silently took her hat from Ellen and placed it back on her head. Her eyes were blazing with fury. Rufus was looking a little sheepish, but Ellen could see the funny side of it all and was biting her lip to stop herself from laughing. It was clear that no one else was going to say anything, so Ellen said, "I'm very sorry."

"Why? What did you do?" said the witch, and marched with a look of thunder to where her spell book lay.

Ellen glanced at Rufus, who winked at her, so she looked away quickly.

Weird Hannah blew some yellow powder off her spell book and found a page towards the end. She sorted out her wand from a pile of spoons and ladles on the floor, then took a handful of blue powder. She let the blue powder slip slowly through her fingers and uttered the words,

> *"Frogs are slimy*
> *Toads are horny*
> *Make Hannah witch-like*
> *Thin and scrawny."*

The powder disappeared in a fountain of blue sparks as it hit the ground. The wand crackled and shook and Hannah started hissing like an untied balloon. She continued hissing until she was suitably skinny again.

Next she touched the cat and mice with her wand and uttered the words,

"O furry friends
Forgive forget
I'll make you normal color yet."

A small flash and a pop saw them right again.

Now Hannah, hands on hips and an indescribable look of witchery on her face, turned to Rufus.

He grinned the sort of grin that shows your teeth but does not make you look happy.

"I told you I could make spells," he said weakly.

But his mother's look was enough to quiet him.

Hannah looked around at the remains of spells all over the floor and walls.

"Worse than the work of goblins," she muttered grimly. She picked up the caldron and put it over the fire to make some more oatmeal. Rufus sat in the upturned table as if it were a boat.

"Sit down," said Weird Hannah to Ellen. "Since you dropped in you may as well stay and have some oatmeal."

But Ellen hated oatmeal.

"No, thank you. I don't like oatmeal," she said.

"Everyone likes oatmeal," snapped the witch.

"Actually, I should be in bed now," Ellen explained. "So I'm not very hungry."

"Whoever goes to bed in the night?" exclaimed Weird Hannah. "You'll be telling me next you go to school during the day."

"People from the real world do go to school during the day," said Rufus brightly, "I read it in a book once."

"And what might you know about the real world?" demanded Weird Hannah.

"She's from the real world," said Rufus, jerking his thumb towards Ellen. And then he added with pride, "I got her here by spell."

Weird Hannah threw both her hands in the air in horror.

"People from the real world in witches' chimneys!" she cried. "Whatever next? When I was a witch girl, witches and people hated each other."

"Oh they still do, mother. They really do," Rufus assured her. "It was a good spell I made, though. And it worked. We can keep her prisoner if you like."

Ellen thought that this had gone on for long enough. She gave a little cough to remind them that she was listening and said, as firmly and politely as possible, "Well, I'm glad I was able to help out. Please don't bother to thank me. It was a pleasure, but I really think I'd better be getting along now, if you could just show me the way back to my bedroom."

Rufus smiled at her and the witch scowled. It was difficult to know how to look back at them.

"We can put her in a cage and take her to the Halloween Revelries," said Rufus.

"Real people aren't allowed at the Revelries," grumbled Weird Hannah.

"We'll tell them she's a witch," said Rufus.

Ellen gave another small cough. The witch poked her in the stomach with her wand.

"Sit-t," said Weird Hannah as if she was talking to a dog. Ellen thought she had better. There was a three-legged stool upside down behind her. She turned it the right way up and sat on it.

Hannah continued, "Now, tell me. What do witches do when they find strange children in their parlors?"

Ellen said she didn't know (although she had a fair idea).

"They put them in cages, or they set them to work," said Rufus gaily.

Weird Hannah looked around at the state of the chimney room.

"Well, we haven't got a cage that's big enough," she said, "so we'll set her to work. She can clean and tidy up in here. She can start after breakfast and have it all spick and span by supper."

Ellen wasn't very pleased at the idea of a cage, but then tidying up had never been one of her favorite pastimes either. In fact, it had caused even more punishments at home, recently, than quarrelling with her brothers, so she realized that she was in a fix. She was sure that some excuse would turn up if she waited long enough, though. It always did.

Rufus began to get ready for Night Witchery classes. He was talking excitedly about Halloween and a big festival held each year by the witch people. It was called the Halloween Revelries. All the local witches and wizards would be there and there would be games and competitions and sideshows.

Ellen thought it sounded much more fun than trick or treat down her street.

"I still think we should take her to the Revelries," Rufus said, and Ellen looked up eagerly.

"She can be one of the sideshows and people can pay to see her," he went on. That didn't sound so good, so Ellen studied the felt tip mark that had got left on her hand from the day before.

"Certainly not!" snapped Weird Hannah, plonking a fresh bowl of steaming oatmeal down on the upturned table for Rufus.

"Now eat!" she ordered.

This time Rufus obeyed. He was feeling good. He had caught a prisoner, he had cast an excellent spell, and he thought that perhaps he had better behave, in case he was banned from the Revelries.

"I'll get my Medallion of Middle Magic tonight, for sure," he said through a mouthful of hot oatmeal.

His Medallion of Middle Magic! Ellen looked up sharply. *She* had a Medallion of Middle Magic in a box on her mantelpiece. She had known from the beginning that it had something to do with the witch in the chimney. Now she could find out how it had appeared so mysteriously and why.

But before Ellen could open her mouth to ask, Weird Hannah, who was smiling a tiny and very rare smile said, "I've polished your Uncle's Medallion of Middle Magic for him, Rufus. It looks beautiful. Would you like to try it on?"

Rufus was cleaning out his oatmeal bowl by running his finger round the rim. He froze for a moment and Ellen noticed that his face had turned faintly green like the oatmeal. Weird Hannah looked in the drawer where she had left the Medallion. The tiny smile disappeared in an instant.

"Funny," she said. "I'm sure I put Uncle's Medallion in the box in the drawer." She started hunting through the things on the floor, then inside cupboards and on shelves.

"It must be here somewhere. Have you seen it, Rufus? Where *is* Uncle's Medallion?" she said.

"Uncle's Medallion?" said Rufus. "Which Uncle? Which Medallion?"

"No, Rufus. Wizard Uncle. Wizard Medallion," said Weird Hannah. "Where is Uncle Whizoon's Medallion?" Steam was coming out of her ears in little puffs.

"Oh, you mean Uncle Whizoon's Medallion of Middle Magic?" said Rufus, as if he had only just understood. Weird Hannah took hold of Rufus's shoulders and shook him until his teeth rattled, and Rufus had the look of someone who was trying hard to remember something. Finally, after much umm-ing and ah-ing and screwing up of his mouth he remembered that he had borrowed the Medallion, the night before, so that he could use it to try out a very special spell.

"But the Medallion makes very powerful magic, very dangerous magic," said Weird Hannah in alarm.

"Yes, it was quite a powerful spell," Rufus admitted.

"And what happened?" whispered Weird Hannah, sitting down on the bed and burying her face in her hands.

"Well, not much, actually," said Rufus. "It's just that the Medallion completely disappeared. I've tried everything and I can't get it back. Something must have gone wrong."

"Wrong! Wrong!" screamed Weird Hannah, jumping to her feet and doing a dance of fury that made her look like the little ballerina on top of Ellen's musical box. "Something has certainly gone wrong! Without that Medallion your Uncle won't take part in the Revelries. Without that Medallion, you will not even *go* to the Revelries! Not this year, or ever again! Something has *certainly* gone wrong!" And with another dance of fury, she raised her eyes to the ceiling, and cried, "What shall I do with the boy? He'll worry me to a shadow. I swear, he'll worry me to a shadow.

And, with that, she pulled her black witch's cloak from a peg on the door, and grabbed her broomstick from the broom cupboard.

"Clear up the mess!" she cried to Ellen. "Or I'll turn you into a frog." Then, turning to Rufus, "You, boy, off to Night Witchery classes. I'm going to see Uncle Whizoon, to find out what can be done."

Muttering crossly to herself, she shot off up the chimney like a rocket, leaving behind her nothing but a cloud of smoke.

4

Ellen at Home

*R*ufus waited until the rocket sound had completely died away, then he winked at Ellen.

"Right," he said. "You'd better get to work. There's a lot of mess to clear up."

But Ellen was not having any of that.

"You made the mess. You clear it up," she said firmly, folding her arms and staying just where she was on the stool. "I'm going home." Rufus's mouth dropped open.

"But you're our prisoner," he said indignantly.

"No, I'm not," Ellen corrected him. "I came here to help

you. You seem to have forgotten that, and anyway," she added with a glint in her eye, "I've got something you want, and you'll have to let me go home to get it."

"I don't believe you," said Rufus. "You're from the real world. What could you possibly have that I might want?"

"You do want to go to the Revelries, I suppose?" asked Ellen, stroking the cat, which had come out of hiding and was brushing to and fro past her legs.

Rufus's face fell. He did want to go to the Halloween Revelries, very badly indeed. He had been planning a wonderful spell for the junior spell competition, and if he won his Medallion of Middle Magic he would join the Grand Order of Middle Magic Makers. That was the burning ambition of all witch boys. Now he had lost his Uncle's Medallion, and he would probably have to wait another whole year. That was unthinkably terrible!

"I know where your Uncle's Medallion is," said Ellen casually.

"Oh, good!" said Rufus, his face bright again with relief. "Have one of these." And he went over to a jar that was lying on the floor. He took the top off and brought out a twisted stick of licorice. All smiles, he handed it to Ellen and said in a coaxing voice, "Now, tell me where the Medallion is."

Ellen loved licorice and would have liked to keep it for later, but she decided it was safer to refuse, so she shook her head and handed it back to Rufus.

"If I bring the Medallion for you, perhaps you can give me something else in return—you know, a wish or something," she said. Rufus looked uneasy.

Ellen went on, "Look, I'll have to fetch the Medallion from home. My mother will never let me out again tonight. Let me go now and I'll bring it for you tomorrow."

Rufus thought while he ate the licorice stick. He looked like a cow chewing cud. The cat leapt onto Ellen's knee and she stroked him until he purred like a pneumatic drill.

Eventually the thoughts in Rufus's mind sorted themselves out into a plan. He said slowly, "You can't come back here during the day, especially before Halloween. It isn't safe. Go now and I'll come to your room in the morning and fetch the Medallion."

Now it was Ellen's turn to be relieved. She suggested that Rufus should help her home as quickly as possible. The sooner she was out of the mess in the parlor the better, she thought, or she might find herself having to tidy up!

There was a great fuss while Rufus sorted through his mother's things to find the book of spells. He needed a rhyme and some powder to get Ellen back to her room. The spell powder he needed had spilled all over the floor so he had to scrape up what he could with a spoon. That being finished, he chose a rhyme from the book and carefully recited the words.

"Bowl of cornflakes
Milk in cup
Be home before
The sun comes up
Marmalade toast
Peanut spread
Go off right now
To your own bed!"

Rufus then let the powder slip through his fingers, which was not easy as it was mixed with tomato ketchup. But he succeeded all the same, and soon, with a sound like rushing water, and a noise like a truck shifting gears on a corner, Ellen felt herself spinning, then found herself upside down in her own bed.

Ellen felt strange, and she had a sense of panic at how little of the night must be left for sleep. She put her head out from under the quilt. She could see through the gap in the yellow curtains that, already, fingers of red were stretching across the sky. She had not, after all, got back before the sun came up. But as she lay, watching the window, silently, an unfamiliar shadow appeared on the window sill in front of the curtain. It stayed on the sill for a moment or two, then jumped down with a soft scuffle. The shadow moved across the room towards her, then leapt on top of her and lay down heavily on her legs. It was purring like a pneumatic drill. Ellen had brought with her, through the spell, the witch's cat!

When she woke up in the morning there was nothing to show for her adventure in the night. Had she really been the prisoner of the witch in the chimney, or had she dreamed it all? She jumped out of bed and ran to the dressing table. There was the box, with the magic signs painted on the lid. She opened it. Inside lay the Medallion, glowing on red velvet. Ellen looked at the pointed hat and words *Medallion of Middle Magic*, and wondered what it all meant.

Just then, Richard knocked on her door on his way down-stairs.

"Get up, lazybones!" he said. "You'll be late."

Ellen could already hear Mom, Dad and Toby downstairs.

"Coming," she called and rushed out of her bedroom to

go to the bathroom. When she came back, she nearly jumped out of her skin. A great big black cat was sitting in the middle of her quilt and washing its ears contentedly.

"Oh, no! I'd forgotten about you," she said. "What *am* I going to do with you?"

With a last look out on the landing, she quickly shut the door.

If the witch cat was really here in the bedroom there could be no doubt that what she thought happened last night, really must have happened. And if it had, then Rufus was really going to visit her today, to collect the Medallion.

"Ellen! Hurry! You'll be late for school!" called Mom from downstairs.

"Coming!" shouted Ellen.

But now she was quite sure of one thing, and that was that she couldn't go to school today. Perhaps she could tell Mom and Dad that there was a holiday, or that she didn't feel well. (She did not feel too marvelous, as a matter of fact.) She pulled her curtain back. It was a bright autumn morning, blue sky above dark red roofs, and the occasional tree covered in golden leaves.

After a search, Ellen at last found her hand mirror under a pile of books. She peered at her face and stuck her tongue out. She didn't look a bit ill. A little tired, perhaps, but that wasn't surprising after all she had been through last night. Well, she decided, there was only one thing to do. She thought of a trick that she had tried before. It hadn't worked then, but this time it might.

Ellen started to jump up and down. Faster and faster she jumped, up and down, round and round. Then she bent down to touch her toes several times. Then she jumped on and off the bed until it shook and squeaked. The cat, who was still sitting on the bed, went up and down as if it was in a boat, and he didn't look pleased.

"Sorry," panted Ellen, and she went on to do some more toe-touching and knee-bending.

Mom called upstairs that Ellen had better come down-stairs this minute and stop banging around before all the plaster came off the ceiling, and Ellen rushed back to her mirror. Her face was now scarlet, and the sweat was running down her forehead like drizzle down a window pane. She was ready.

She staggered down to breakfast without bothering to put on a bathrobe and looking as miserable as she could. Toby was making a fuss because he did not want his Rice Krispies. Dad and Richard were just finishing plates of bacon and eggs.

Richard was having a special breakfast this morning because he was taking his music exam.

Ellen's Rice Krispies were already in her bowl, crackling like a witch's spell. She sat down in front of them, looking forlorn, and whispered, "I can't. I just can't." Then she had a good cough and looked at Mom.

"Good Heavens!" said Mom. "You look terrible. Back to bed immediately. No school for you today, I'm afraid."

"She's bewitched, I expect," said Richard. "Wish me luck, El, and ask your magical friends to make a spell for me, to help me through the exam." Ellen looked at her bowl and said nothing.

"You go back to bed," said Dad, and he kissed her good-bye.

"Goodbye," said Ellen weakly.

"Wish me good luck," said Richard again.

"Good luck," murmured Ellen, but her fingers were crossed under the table and she did not mean it.

Mom and Toby saw Dad and Richard off, but Ellen stayed at the table. She was really very hungry, but she dared not show it. It would spoil her plan. When Mom and Toby came back into the kitchen, Ellen crawled upstairs, and then, arriving in her room, hopped nimbly into bed.

The witch cat was waiting for her and began to purr loudly.

"So, when is Rufus coming back for the Medallion?" Ellen asked him, but the cat had just found an itch on its back and turned to bite it hard, then carried on purring.

"You like it here, don't you?" said Ellen, stroking him. She hopped out of bed to get the gold box, and put it on the pillow beside her. "Do you think I'll get a wish for returning the Medallion, puss?" she asked the cat. The cat may have nodded. "I shall wish that Richard fails his exam and doesn't have to go away. Then he can stay at home, where he belongs. I won't give them the Medallion back, unless they give me a wish."

Mom called up to see whether Ellen would like breakfast in bed. Ellen said, "Yes," and tried not to sound too eager. She put the cat in the closet, and told it not to purr too loudly and hid the gold box under her quilt. When Mom came upstairs with Ellen's breakfast, she took her temperature, and said that she had better have some medicine and a nap. Ellen nodded obediently, took the medicine and asked Toby not to play airplanes outside her room. She ate her breakfast, put the tray on the floor, and let her head sink into the pillow.

There was a short break while Ellen sat cross-legged on the bed, thinking about the wish she was going to ask for. She was very excited.

Then she heard the words, almost inside her head.

"Howl and thud
And sonic boom
Take me now
To Ellen's room."

And there, in a shower of silver sparks and a cloud of green smoke, appeared Rufus, with a look of amazement on his face.

"I told you I could do spells," he said.

Now, had he arrived on his own, things might have been different, but for some reason, Rufus had brought with him his mother's broomstick. It was huge and powerful and Ellen's room was not really big enough for it. As Rufus turned to look around him one end of the stick swung round and there was a terrible crashing sound of things being swept off shelves.

"Oh, dear. I'm sorry," said Rufus, not looking at all sorry and, as he stepped backwards to look at the damage, he stuck the handle of the broom through the closed window.

The cat ran under the bed. It was used to this sort of thing. There was a loud musical smashing sound, as the glass in the window shattered.

"Oh, dear. I'm sorry," said Rufus again.

Ellen was watching, horrified.

"Just look what you've done!" she cried.

Rufus gave an embarrassed laugh.

"Never mind that," he said, pointing with his thumb to the broken window. "I know someone who can fix that in a trice."

"In a trice?" said Ellen. "What if my mother comes up here in half a trice?" As they gazed through the jagged hole, the last pieces of glass tinkled to the ground.

"Has something broken?" called Mom from below.

"It'll be all right," replied Ellen hopefully. Fortunately, Mom did not come up.

"Well?" demanded Ellen, looking at the witch boy. "How are we going to fix the window in a trice?" And then she took the opportunity to say that she would not return the Medallion unless the window was good as new, and added gingerly that she would like a wish too.

"We'll have to see about that," said Rufus, winking and

climbing astride the broom. "But, first, we'll get the spell to mend the window. . . ."

"In a trice," Ellen joined in, and then she snapped. "And stop winking at me. I don't like it."

"Get on the stick behind me," said Rufus, twisting around and knocking Ellen's jigsaw flying with the broom handle.

Ellen bundled some clothes under her quilt so her mother would think she was sleeping if she looked in and then she climbed aboard.

Here goes, she thought.

Rufus had some powder in his pocket. He took out a handful and let it slip through his fingers.

> *"Black night*
> *Light day*
> *Old witch folk say*
> *Up, up, away!"*

he said clearly. Then he made three circles in the air with his hand, tapped the broomstick twice and off they flew, through the gaping window.

It was like sitting on a firework rocket gone mad. There

was a whooshing, fizzing sound. The cold air whipped past them, then they were way up above the rooftops of the long row of houses.

I shall be sick, thought Ellen as they circled higher and higher. But she wasn't, and in time she began to enjoy herself.

"Wow!" she cried on a downward swoop, as her stomach turned over and over; she was riding the biggest rollercoaster in the world. "This is fantastic!"

Rufus made for a cluster of gray rooftops, a few streets away. They touched down by a tall narrow chimney. Ellen climbed off the broomstick as she would climb off a bike with a crossbar.

"Woweee!" was all she could say.

"Follow me," said Rufus, also climbing off the broomstick, and propping it up on end. Then he hopped inside the chimney pot and disappeared from view. Ellen followed as quickly as she could. She slid down through the chimney, down, down and down, until, at last, she landed heavily at the bottom. She was in a long room that looked like a miniature hospital ward. It was lit by tiny candles burning at each bedside. She was just struggling to her feet, when a mug, dropping dregs of cocoa, came hurtling past her left ear, just missing her and smashing on the wall behind.

"This is a goblin dormitory," explained Rufus. "Good Witching," he said cheerfully to somebody small who lay asleep beneath a patchwork quilt, on one of the beds. All Ellen could see was the top of a head.

"Lorluvvagoblin. It's the middle of the day," gabbled a small voice.

"Lorluvvagoblin it's the middle of the day," chorused several voices from under covers in different parts of the room.

"We need to speak to you. We need a spell urgently," said Rufus, throwing back the patchwork quilt to reveal a goblin, curled up so tightly that it was hard to tell which end was which. The goblin's wiry arm grabbed the bedside clock and hurled it at Rufus.

"Missed," said Rufus, ducking.

"Return in night shadows," sang other little voices from around the room.

"Yes, return in night shadows," said the first goblin, burying himself again under the patchwork quilt.

"We can't. We need a spell and it's urgent," said Rufus. "Have a cup of cocoa." He went across the room to where there was a little stove, and put the kettle on to boil.

"Goblins always feel better after something hot," he explained to Ellen.

The goblin under the patchwork quilt was called Bobgoblin. When he got out of bed to drink his cocoa, Ellen could see that he was a fat little creature with skinny arms and legs, and wearing a red nightshirt. The other goblins stayed tucked up in their beds.

Bobgoblin drank the cocoa noisily.

"Good Witching," he said, when he had finished drinking, and wiped his mouth on his sleeve. "So you want one of Bobgoblin's spells, do you?" he went on.

"Yes, please," said Rufus.

"*Return in night shadows. Return in night shadows,*" sang the other goblins.

"Rufus broke my bedroom window," explained Ellen, trying to ignore the voices from the other beds.

"A smashed window, yippeee!" said Bobgoblin, hurling his cocoa mug across the room where it broke into pieces. "A smashed window, goblins! Did you hear that?"

"*A smashed window. A smashed window,*" chorused the others.

"Goblins smash and mend things," Rufus explained to Ellen.

"We hoped you might fix the window for us," Ellen told Bobgoblin.

"She's from the real world," Rufus explained to the goblin, as if it were only people from the real world who worried about such things as broken windows. Bobgoblin's little face uncreased and his smile disappeared.

"But goblins don't like people from the real world," he said.

"People from the real world should stay in the real world," muttered the other goblins.

"I know, but she's not too bad," said Rufus, pointing at Ellen with his thumb. "She's just a bit ignorant. She's got my Uncle's Medallion, and she wants a wish in return for giving it back. She may have to come to the Halloween Revelries."

If Bobgoblin's face had fallen before, it practically slid down his fat stomach now.

"Real people at the Revelries!" he said. "By the great Wizard of Ages Ago. *Real* people aren't allowed at the Revelries!"

"Real people at the Revelries," chorused the goblins.

"We'll say she's a witch," said Rufus.

The goblin hopped from foot to foot, uneasily.

"A witch. A witch. She looks not like a witch," he said.

"She's really not like a person from the real world at all," said Rufus. "She gets up at night, and joins in spells. It'll be all right," he promised. But Bobgoblin was still not sure. He came up very close to Rufus and looked all around him as he spoke in a whisper.

"The Hideous Halloween Haunters. What about the Hideous Halloween Haunters?" he said.

There was a shivering and a shaking but no words from the other goblins in the beds.

"Oh, she's not afraid of them," said Rufus brightly.

"No, I'm not afraid of them because I've never heard of them," said Ellen shortly. She got fed up with these conversations when people talked about her as if she wasn't there.

Rufus had to make Bobgoblin some more cocoa, and when he had drunk the cocoa and smashed the mug, the goblin's spirits revived.

"All will be well. All will be well," he said. "And now about the broken window."

"*The window! The window! Get on with the dratted window*," came the voices from the beds, and Bobgoblin set about finding a spell for Ellen and Rufus.

Bobgoblin's spell books were kept in a locker by his bed. They were paperbacks and rather dog-eared. Bobgoblin pulled one book out and all the others fell on the floor. He hunted among them for some wire spectacles, which he found eventually and put on. He looked through the first book he had found, then, getting to the page he wanted, he read out:

"Broken windows. Now, let me see. Broken attic windows. Broken bus windows. Broken car windows. No, here it is. Broken bedroom windows. You need a pane of glass, some putty, a ladder and a handyman." And he looked up over his spectacles. "But that's not quite what you had in mind, of course."

"Not quite," admitted Ellen. "It's just with you being a goblin and everything, we thought that there might be a way of mending the window in a trice."

"Mmmmm," said the goblin, deep in thought. Then he read, "In cases of extreme urgency, try the following. . . . Utter the words,

> *Swoop low over water*
> *Sail through the sky*
> *Tap twice on the window*
> *In a trice fix the window*
> *While broomsticking by.*

1. Apply powder (mud-colored, medium strength). 2. Follow instructions in rhyme. 3. Hope very hard."

Bobgoblin shut the book, removed his spectacles, did a quick dance and giggled a quick giggle, at which there was a chorus of *"Come back in night shadows."*

"Is that what you wanted?" asked Bobgoblin, hopping about all over the place and then jumping up and down on his bed.

"Yes, I think so," said Ellen, trying to follow him with her eyes. It was hard talking to someone so lively. Bobgoblin took some mud-colored powder from an envelope which he had in another drawer of the locker and gave it to Rufus.

"Take care," he said. "Now be off with you and return in night shadows."

"Yes, I will," said Ellen. "Thank you."

"Good Witching, Bobgoblin," said Rufus.

And Bobgoblin took all the books out of his locker and threw them up in the air, so that the pages fluttered down everywhere.

"Goblins love breaking and mending," Rufus reminded Ellen.

"Yes. I can see," said Ellen. "Thank you Bobgoblin. Good Witching."

"*Good Witching! Good Witching!*" came from all the little beds and Bobgoblin threw himself back into his bed and curled up tightly. Ellen replaced the patchwork quilt and followed Rufus back up the chimney.

6
A Swim

They arrived back in the brightness of the rooftop where they had left the broomstick leaning against the chimney, and climbed aboard again. Rufus repeated the flying spell, and they were off. Away they flew across the roofs and roads, coming down a little lower to watch the cars running to and fro, like toy cars on a track. They detoured around some huge office buildings and peeped in at the windows as they passed, and then flew high above Ellen's school where they could see children drifting out of the building for recess. Ellen waved and shouted but no one looked up. If only she could find the place where Richard was taking his music exam, she thought, she would do her best to distract him. But she was not sure how to find him.

"We'd better get back to that window of yours," Rufus said at last.

"Yes, we'd better," Ellen agreed.

"First we have to swoop low over water," said Rufus.

"Swoop low over water
Sail through the sky
Tap thrice on the window
In a trice mend the window
While broomsticking by."

They rehearsed the poem together until they were sure they had got it right.

"There's a pond in the park," suggested Ellen.

"Of course!" said Rufus, snapping his fingers. "At nightime we fly over the park and the pond looks just like glass! Hold tight!"

And off they sped.

Soon they arrived at the park and could see the pond below. It had a jetty running into it and it looked a bit like a wonky ping-pong paddle. As well as the open parkland, where people were walking their dogs and sitting on benches, there were clumps of trees and bushes. They were all different colors at this time of year; gold, red, orange, brown, and some were still green. There were trees and bushes clustered around the pond.

With a shout of glee, Rufus directed the broomstick sharply downwards into the trees. As he did so, he threw himself off the broomstick and onto a branch. He hung there, like a monkey at the zoo, laughing and kicking his feet. Ellen was left alone on the broomstick which flew upwards again.

"Rufus!" screamed Ellen angrily. "Rufus! Bring me back down immediately! Don't leave me!"

"Just raise your right elbow to go left, and your left elbow to go right," called Rufus, by now a small voice in the distance.

Ellen wobbled furiously, looped the loop, came within inches of flying into a bush, but finally brought the broomstick past the tree where she had begun. Her heart was beating like a drum. Rufus grabbed hold of the passing broomstick and pulled himself aboard in full flight. The two of them circled round again.

"By the Revelries, you'll be good enough to race," said Rufus. "You make a very good witch!"

"I don't want to be a witch," snapped Ellen, "and I won't give you back the Medallion, either, if you play any more tricks! That could have been very dangerous." And she hung on tightly, with her arms around Rufus's waist, to make sure he did not go away again. But Rufus was now deep in thought.

"Swoop low over water," he said. "That won't be easy with all these trees. If it looks as if we're going to crash, we'll have to make a jump for it."

"Without a parachute?" said Ellen.

But Rufus was concentrating and didn't reply. The next thing Ellen knew, they were soaring above the trees again, then they were heading fast downwards, making straight for the glistening water.

"Feet up!" cried Rufus, as the water seemed to race up to meet them. Ellen felt her feet break the surface of the water and carve a long straight furrow through it. Then she felt the stick begin to shudder and zig-zag. Suddenly the trees ahead were coming at them at a terrifying speed.

"I can't get the stick up again!" screamed Rufus. "We're going to crash! Quick, jump before it's too late! *Jump!*"

So Ellen jumped.

Rufus held his nose and plunged after Ellen into the pond. The broomstick continued on course for the trees. Its swishing, fizzing sound ended with a sickening thud, and two clunks, as it fell in half. Then all went quiet.

The pond water was not as cold as Ellen had expected. She seemed to go down a very long way beneath the surface, round and round in the grayness. There were green plants waving at her as she passed and the occasional fish flitted by on its way to keep an appointment. She began to wish that she could take a breath, but there was nothing but murky water all around her. Her chest felt tight and uncomfortable. She was just beginning to fear that she would never come up again when she felt a strong bony hand grip her wrist. Rufus, swimming like a frog, was pulling her up and up, and at last she found herself back at the surface of the pond.

Ellen took a huge breath and must have swallowed some water because she started coughing and spluttering. Rufus gave her an enormous punch on the back, which pushed her back under the water. He yanked her up again by her sweater. Ellen spluttered, "Thank you," but did not mean it.

"Don't mention it." Rufus beamed. His eyes were completely covered by his hair, which was flattened down over his face. He pushed it back, and Ellen was afraid for a minute that he was going to wink. They swam or rather splashed their way to the edge of the pond, and staggered up the bank. After a moment's rest, when they were both too winded to say anything, they decided that there was no time to lose and that they had better go and hunt for the broomstick. They discovered it among the trees, broken in two.

Rufus and Ellen were wet and cold and their teeth were chattering.

"P-p-perhaps we can ride a piece each," suggested Ellen, looking down at the broken broomstick.

"N-n-no such luck," said Rufus. "Broken broomsticks don't fly."

They crouched down under the trees to examine the pieces of stick, with puddles forming around their feet.

"W-well, we'll just have to walk home," said Ellen sensibly.

Rufus did not like that idea at all. Witch boys did not walk around in the daytime, he said, and it wasn't very often that they walked at night.

"I'll get us back by broomstick one way or another," said Rufus. "Follow me." And with that he picked up the bristle end of the broomstick and set off through the trees. Ellen picked up the handle end and followed. Rufus made his way to a grounds keeper's shed in a clearing. He opened the door and went inside to have a look around. Ellen stood outside, dripping wet, and wondering why there was nobody else around. At last, Rufus emerged from the shed looking thoroughly pleased with himself and carrying an ordinary modern floor broom with a very long handle.

"Let's try with this," he said.

"But it doesn't even look right!" Ellen laughed. "Whoever heard of a witch flying around on one of these?"

"Well, there's got to be a first time," said Rufus, so they left the old broken broomstick in the shed, and took the ordinary broom with them to a bigger clearing.

Amid fits of giggles, they got astride the broom and tried to take to the sky again.

> *"Black night*
> *Light day*
> *Old witch folk*
> *Say*
> *Up up away,"*

they tried to say, but they were laughing so much that they could scarcely get it out and had to try again. Then Rufus tried to drop some magic powder between his fingers. What actually happened was that a hard lump of stuck-together powder plopped onto the ground.

"This is never going to work in a hundred years!" said Ellen, wet all over, with tears of laughter pouring down her cheeks.

"Shh! I'm concentrating," said Rufus, pulling himself together and taking on a very serious look.

When the spell still refused to work, Ellen said, "Why don't we just walk home?"

But Rufus wouldn't give in. One day, he planned to be a great wizard, and he had no intention of being beaten by a broken broomstick. Anyway, he didn't know how he was going to explain all this to his mother. The broken broomstick was one thing, arriving home on foot and empty-handed was another.

"Try sitting the other way," he said to Ellen.

So Ellen turned round the other way, but she found it very hard to take this flight seriously.

"We must look so funny." She giggled. "If only Richard could see me now. Oh, no, I'm going to sneeze. Probably the beginning of a terrible cold. I am . . . I'm going to sneeze, watch out . . . a-a-a-tishoooooooo!"

Ellen was famed throughout her class at school for the force of her sneezes, but this was an extra special one. Just as if a rocket had fired all its engines. The grounds keeper's broom was blasted off by the sneeze. Whoosh! It soared above the trees, straight up in the air, Rufus and Ellen hanging on for all they were worth.

"I told you I could do spells!" cried Rufus in glee.

"I never thought a sneeze could do that!" shouted Ellen.

"With your sneezes and my spells we can do anything!" said Rufus, and Ellen really felt as though it was true.

They made a huge white circle against the autumn sky and set off for the nearby rooftops and home.

7

The Window

*E*llen's house was the fourth from the end of the row of houses on her street. The sky had become overcast, and Ellen was worried that it might begin to rain before the window was fixed. Together they rehearsed the spell once more.

They did three circles past the window, tapping the frame each time. As they circled a fourth time, Rufus sprinkled some of the magic powder which had now dried out in his pocket. Like a film running backwards, the glass flew up from the ground and from the window sill. There was a musical tinkling sound as the glass pieces came back to-gether. The window was as good as new.

Rufus could not believe his luck. He had never done so many spells right in such a short space of time before. He was getting to like Ellen more every minute. He looked at her proudly, waiting for a compliment.

"Yes. It was very good," said Ellen.

They circled around again admiringly.

"By the way," said Ellen, into Rufus's ear, "now the win-dow is whole again, just how am I supposed to get back inside?"

"I'm glad you asked that," said Rufus.

"Well?" asked Ellen.

"I'm glad you asked that, but I don't know the answer," said Rufus with one of his irritating winks. They flew one more time around a television aerial, then landed on the roof to think about it.

They sat huddled damply together by a chimney. The weather was turning grayer and grayer, Rufus had to admit that he still hadn't had an idea. He explained that it was be-cause he was getting tired.

"Well, let's get the spell book again," said Ellen. "We're near your chimney and it's going to rain."

Rufus wasn't too eager to take Ellen into his chimney again, especially during the day. Weird Hannah had not exactly liked Ellen, and the witch was even more crabby in the day than she was at night.

"We'll be very quiet," said Ellen, for the wind was now blowing harder and she was cold.

Rufus shrugged.

"Well, all right," he said reluctantly. "Follow me." He ran nimbly up the roof, and Ellen had to follow as well as she could, on her hands and knees. She was not as used to this as he was. Rufus jumped onto the chimney Ellen had fallen down the night before.

"Shh!" said Rufus loudly. "She changes people into frogs when she's in a *good* mood. When she's in a *bad* mood, she changes them into head lice."

Ellen shuddered.

"We'll be *very* quiet," she said. They climbed inside the chimney pot and slid down into the parlor.

Rufus landed lightly and Ellen, with a bump, on top of him. Rufus pushed her off and they stood up. The parlor was neat and tidy now. There was no sign of the chaos in the night, except for a few spell stains on the walls. A caldron of something hot was bubbling nicely over the fire. Ellen decided not to ask what it was in case it turned out to be green oatmeal again. She was hungry but she wanted her dinner at home. The table, now the right way up, was laid for breakfast. Weird Hannah was fast asleep in a bed at one side of the parlor. She was snoring gently, and two mice, sharing a crust of bread on top of her, were going up and down as she breathed.

"Shhh!" said Rufus to the mice.

The mice stopped eating just for a moment and looked up.

The spell book lay on the table.

"Look," said Rufus, who had started a fit of yawning. "I'm really not in the mood for all this at the moment. I'm very tired. I wonder if we could wait until. . . ."

"No. I have to get back home now," said Ellen firmly. "What about my mother?"

"What about mine?" said Rufus gloomily and he yawned another enormous yawn. It sounded like the brakes of an eighteen-wheeler.

Weird Hannah stirred. Rufus and Ellen looked at her silently, then at each other.

"I'm so tired," whispered Rufus eventually. "After all it is the middle of the day."

"I know. Just one more spell . . ." began Ellen, but before

she knew what was happening, Rufus had curled up around the table leg and fallen fast asleep.

"Wake up! Wake up!" said Ellen, shaking him furiously. But once Rufus was asleep, he was asleep. He had a happy peaceful look on his face as he hugged the table leg. Weird Hannah stirred again and turned right over and the mice took their meal elsewhere.

"I always knew I couldn't really trust him," said Ellen shaking her head. She sighed deeply and wondered what she could do next. It didn't take her long to make up her mind that she was going home for her dinner, Rufus or no Rufus. She knew that her room was only on the other side of the wall by Rufus's bed. It surely could not be too difficult to get back there without the aid of a spell. She would climb back over the roof and down a drainpipe, like children did in stories. That way she only risked breaking her neck. If she stayed here until Weird Hannah woke up, she might be turned into a head louse.

Ellen took one last look around, then prepared to leave.

8

Ellen on the Roof

*E*llen's jeans and sweater were still a little damp, so she decided to borrow a black cloak that she found hanging on the back of a cupboard door. She threw it around her shoulders and fastened it at the neck. At least she wouldn't freeze to death. She was getting quite good at scrambling up and down chimneys, so she decided to leave the way she had entered. She found footholds in the walls, and she knew that she was as good a tree climber as anyone in the real world, so she began to climb up. But she had more the feeling of going up in an elevator than climbing a chimney. She must have been helped by the witch's cloak.

Eventually her head popped out of the chimney pot, but the sky was now very overcast, and it was a dismal world up here on the roof. There seemed to be acres and acres of roof-tops and the grays and reds seemed to merge together. The tree tops were losing more leaves all the time as the wind blew through them. Birds huddled on television aerials, and chimneys stood in silent rows like soldiers.

Ellen worked her way carefully across the roof and around another chimney. She could see a man on top of a nearby warehouse, fixing the roof. She waved and shouted but the man did not look up from his work. She found a gable and sat astride it so that she could take a better look below. Every-thing down there was as it usually was. The thought struck Ellen that people would think it funny, seeing her perched on a gable, like a pigeon, but no one seemed to notice.

She set about looking for a good strong drainpipe that she could slide down to the ground. She followed the rain-gutter until she found one, but it looked very flimsy and she only had to put her foot onto it to make it wobble. These houses had three stories, so it was a long climb down. Ellen knew that if she did not find a really strong drainpipe she was going to fall and break her neck. She was beginning to think that, after all, she might prefer to become a head louse. She decided that she would just have to look for help. You could move for miles on the roofs around here because the houses were all connected in a long row, and the roofs went up and down like pointed sand dunes. She set off to explore.

But running up and down roofs was much more difficult, even, than running over sand dunes where the sand is soft and deep. It felt to Ellen like running in a dream, when you desperately want to get somewhere, but your feet somehow get stuck at every step. Up and down Ellen ran, until she did not know what she was looking for any more, or, for that matter, where she was. She was cold and alone, and it was beginning to rain. She thought she saw a very large bird fly over her, like an airplane. Her legs were hurting and she was getting wet. She came to the edge of a roof where she could look down on a road she did not recognize, and sat down and wrapped her cloak around her and wondered what would become of her.

As she watched the people moving busily below, she found she was watching one person in particular. With a little shock of delight, she realized it was Richard. He had his violin with him and had obviously just finished his music exam and was on the way back to school.

"Help! Help!" she cried at the top of her voice. "It's me, Ellen. I'm stuck on the roof!"

He did not look up. No one in the street looked up. Without a glance in her direction, Richard turned a corner and disappeared from view. Ellen was bitterly disappointed. Tears pricked her eyes.

"Don't go, Richard," she murmured sadly. "Please don't go." But he had gone and there was nothing she could do about it.

"Well, anyone!" shouted Ellen. "Can anyone down there help me? I want to go home."

Still no one looked up. Ellen was *furious*. She could hear them. Why couldn't they hear her? She was sad and *furious* and hungry, and, since she did not know what else to do, she sat down just where she was and cried as if her heart would break.

"Cheer up, little lass," said a deep voice. "Things can't be as bad as all that."

Ellen looked around to see two enormous hobnailed boots,

swinging as if they were on two ropes, coming down the roof towards her. With two thumps, they came to rest beside her.

"Yes, things are as bad as that," said Ellen. "I'm very, very hungry!"

"Do you always cry when you're hungry?" asked the voice.

"No," said Ellen. "I don't. But I'm cold and wet too. And fed up, and I want to go home." She looked all around her, then went on, "Anyway, who are you? Where are you? I can't see you."

"Well, you're a funny little witch and no mistake," said the voice. "Fancy expecting to be able to see a ghost in the daytime."

"You're a ghost!" exclaimed Ellen.

"Yes. Here I am. I've got my boots on," he said.

"A ghost with boots on!" said Ellen, a smile creeping right across her face. She was quite cheered up by the thought.

"Now, I didn't come here to be laughed at," moaned the ghost. "There may not be much to me during the day, but I do a very good glow at night. A very good glow indeed."

"Oh, I wasn't laughing at you," said Ellen quickly. "Really, I wasn't. I'm glad to see you. That is . . . I mean . . . I'm glad to meet you. I'm Ellen, from the real world."

"O'Glow. Extra Bright O'Glow's the name," said the ghost. "My friends call me Extra Bright." Ellen felt a coldness stretch out towards her hand. She thought it must be a ghostly handshake. Extra Bright went on.

"From the real world, you say? You're from the real world? You shouldn't be out here on your own, little lass. It isn't safe."

"I can't help it. I came here by spell and I'm stuck," said Ellen shortly.

Just then a dark shadow passed over them like an enormous bird.

"Whatever was that?" asked Ellen.

"That's one of the Hideous Halloween Haunters. They pick children off the rooftops, like eagles catching rabbits," said Extra Bright. "It's not safe for people from the real world up here."

"Well, I was hoping that you might be able to help me get back home again," said Ellen.

"Back to the real world?" moaned the ghost, and he added a very small howl. "Oh dear, I'm not too sure about that. There's not much magic about during the day."

Ellen felt Extra Bright's coldness come closer to her, but she tried not to shiver because she didn't want to hurt his feelings again. He was the kindest thing that she had met since her adventure began, and she didn't want him to go away. Extra Bright's boots were now resting in the guttering beside her canvas shoes, and she knew the ghost was sitting beside her, even though she could not see him. It was like having a conversation on the telephone, talking to someone you couldn't see.

Extra Bright told her that he was here for the Halloween Revelries, and had nowhere to stay, which was why he was drifting around rooftops during the day. But, he added, sounding a little like Ellen's headmaster, there was no excuse for a child like Ellen to be doing the same. He thought that the Hideous Halloween Haunter might have seen her, and, between them, Ellen and Extra Bright decided that it would be safer to find somewhere sheltered to stay until nightfall, and then they could arrange Ellen's return.

The hobnail boots got up and swung off up the roof. Ellen climbed to her feet and followed. They went to a small group of chimneys that stood together like a three-walled house. Extra Bright took Ellen's witch's cloak and threw it across the chimneys to make a roof.

"The Halloween Haunters are down here for the Revelries too," Extra Bright explained when he and Ellen were safe inside the tent. "Usually they live a long way off in the land of Nightmares."

"Oh, I see," said Ellen, remembering how frightened the goblins had been at the mention of the Halloween Haunters. "But, you see, the reason all this started is that I have Uncle Whizoon's Medallion of Middle Magic, and I want to go to the Revelries to return it to him. I think I'm going to get a wish."

The ghost did a series of howls.

"Real people at the Revelries," he murmured dolefully. "It isn't allowed."

"But I really do need a wish," said Ellen. "Or my brother might have to go away."

"That's sad," said Extra Bright. "Very sad."

"If I can get home. Get the Medallion. Get my wish, then everything will be all right," said Ellen.

Just then her stomach rumbled furiously, she was so hungry.

"If you don't get something to eat," said Extra Bright, changing the subject, "you'll soon be too weak to go to the Revelries, or any other place for that matter."

Ellen nodded her head, because that was just how she felt herself. Extra Bright was most understanding.

"I'll find you something to eat," said Extra Bright.

"Not oatmeal?" said Ellen suspiciously.

"Not oatmeal," said Extra Bright. "I shall drift into the real world and find a refrigerator. A full refrigerator. There is no refrigerator in the real world that can keep me out, especially if I leave my boots behind." Ellen's eyes brightened again.

"Ooh, yes," she said with enthusiasm. And, with that, the cold feeling, which had the beginnings of a glow in the gloom, left the little tent between chimneys. The boots, however, stayed behind.

Ellen did not know how long she waited for Extra Bright to return, but, eventually, a package of cheese and onion flavored crackers sailed into the tent, followed by some chocolate chip cookies and, last of all, a can of cola with a straw. Extra Bright was, without doubt, the nicest ghost she had ever met.

When she was full she did not care how gray and miserable it was outside. She was warm and dry and she chatted happily to Extra Bright and exchanged ghost stories with him until late afternoon. Then they both fell asleep.

9

Fetching the Medallion

When Ellen woke up, the cloak had been removed from over the chimneys, and she was looking up at a clear night sky. Stars were scattered everywhere, like confetti on the carpet after Toby's birthday party. Ellen could hear voices all around her. She sat up and rubbed her eyes.

> *"When a child awakes*
> *With stars in its eyes*
> *Goblins warn*
> *That come the morn*

That child will not
With joy arise,"

sang a little voice that sounded like a record put on at the wrong speed.

"Quiet, Bobgoblin," said another, that sounded like a tape recorder run too slowly.

The voices belonged to Bobgoblin and Extra Bright O'Glow. They were standing looking at Ellen and waiting for her to wake up.

"Is she awake?" said Rufus. "Oh good. Now we can send her back for the Medallion."

He joined the ghost and the goblin, standing over Ellen, and Bobgoblin danced around a chimney and back again.

Ellen smiled and stood up. She stretched and looked around. She could see other goblins, ghosts and witch people all over the roof tops. In the moonlight she noticed that they were busily preparing for something.

"They're getting ready for the Halloween Revelries," Extra Bright explained. He was now a towering glow against the sky. He was right. He did do a good glow at night.

"You must go and get the Medallion quickly," said Rufus, taking hold of Ellen's arm.

"Medallions, Medallions, many Medallions
By wizards and witch children, there to be won.
Medallions, Medallions, many Medallions
In rain, clouds or moonlight e're Halloween's done,"

sang Bobgoblin and he scuttled around Ellen's legs.

"I have a wonderful spell for the spell competition, especially if it rains," said Rufus excitedly. "Quick! Back you go for the Medallion."

Ellen was not too sure where she had to go or how she had to get there, so she looked at Extra Bright, who was hovering around and trying to calm everyone down.

"Are you ready to go back for the Medallion?" Extra Bright asked Ellen.

Ellen looked at Rufus. He was anxiously looking over his shoulder to make sure that his mother did not catch him, but his face was bright with expectation. He had been waiting for a very long time to win his own Medallion. So Ellen decided to forget how cross she had been with him for falling asleep and stranding her here on the roof. A few hours earlier she would have gladly thrown the Medallion into the pond in the park and never returned it. But now the Halloween Revelries were beginning, and there was a sense of great excitement everywhere. She did not want to miss the Revelries, and she certainly did not want to miss having her wish granted.

"Yes, I'm ready," she said.

"*A spell, a spell, and all is well*," sang Bobgoblin.

"I'll do the spell," said Rufus, waving his arms about in magical motions.

"Not so fast. Not so fast," said Extra Bright, thoughtfully. "We have to get Ellen to the real world, then we have to get her back to the rooftops. The spell must be done well. We don't want to risk losing her, or the Medallion, in between." Everyone agreed, especially Ellen.

After a great deal of discussion, it was decided that everyone would pool their power to make a special spell. Ellen would be able to go back to her room in the real world and collect the Medallion. When she was ready, she would be able to restart the spell herself. Bobgoblin would sing the spell to send her off, Rufus would do the bit with the powder, Extra Bright would stand by. Ellen would restart the spell by saying the words "Let the spell begin" when it was necessary. She would be returned home and then to the same place on the roof as soon as possible. It seemed that nothing could go wrong.

It took another few minutes with heads together and some argument to produce the spell rhyme that would be most suitable for this occasion. In the end, the rhyme that they agreed on was this one.

Return, return
As seconds tick
On watches and on clocks.
Return, return
Blinking quick
Medallion bring
In box.

Rufus had some powder left over from previous spells in his pocket. He stood with a grand expression on his face, ready to throw the powder. Bobgoblin called some of his goblin friends over to help sing the rhyme. He said it would sound better. Extra Bright hovered and gave advice. Ellen was glad he was there. She found a high place to stand on the roof, closed her eyes and gritted her teeth.

The goblins gave a fine performance of the rhyme. Rufus sprinkled the powder with a magnificent flourish. Extra

Bright said, "Off you go, little lass. Be back soon," and Ellen felt herself drifting into the blackness that she knew would bring her back to the real world.

She concentrated hard and wondered whether anyone was going to believe any of this when she told them, or whether they would all tell her she had been dreaming. She wondered if . . . she wondered if. . . . Thoughts drifted through her mind like sheep through a gate and then with a start, she opened her eyes. She was back at home.

Ellen found herself in the kitchen downstairs. Could no one up there ever get a spell right? She let herself out. Everything was dark. She crept upstairs. The family had already come up for bed. Ellen stopped at Richard's door. She could hear him turning the pages of a book and knew that he was still awake. Forgetting how annoyed she had been with him earlier, she burst into his room.

"Richard, Richard, you must come with me," she said in a loud whisper.

Richard looked up in surprise.

"Oh, so you're awake at last, are you?" he said.

"I'm going to have a fantastic adventure on the roof," Ellen went on. "There's going to be witches and goblins and ghosts, a sort of big party in the sky. It's Halloween!"

"Go with you to the roof? Ellen, don't be silly. It's the middle of the night," Richard said.

"I know it is, but you must come. I'm going to get a wish. I shall wish that you have to stay here and not go away."

"I said, don't be silly, El," snapped Richard. "You know I want to go."

"If I wish for you to stay," said Ellen wickedly, "something will go wrong. You won't be able to go."

"Don't you dare!" said Richard. He aimed his book at her as if he meant to throw it.

"Come with me and you can have the wish instead," bargained Ellen, looking at him hopefully.

Richard sighed, turned his back on her and slid deeper down into bed.

"Go away, frog face, I'm tired," he said. "And you're crazy. Go back to bed."

"I'm going to the roof," Ellen whispered, "I'm going alone. I'll wish that everything goes wrong for you, and that you fail your rotten exam, so there!"

She flounced out of Richard's room and into her own bedroom. The black cat was still curled up on the yellow cover of her unmade bed. It looked up, blinking, and trying to get used to the light.

"I must take you back with me this time," she said in a whisper and the cat purred, but she had no time to stroke it now.

The gold box was under the quilt, just as she had left it. She hastily checked to see that the Medallion of Middle Magic was still inside. It lay on the velvet with its heavy gold chain. At night it seemed to glow like a light under water. It was very beautiful.

Ellen knew she had to get back quickly or the Revelries would have already begun. She picked up the cat and held it awkwardly in one arm. She carried the box in the other hand.

"Right. Now I'm ready," she whispered. "Let the spell begin." She was just beginning to get the strange dizzy feeling that she got with spells, when her bedroom door clicked open.

Richard! thought Ellen. He must have changed his mind!

But as the door opened further and a head peered around it, Ellen could see that it was not Richard, but Toby.

"Oh, no, Toby! Go back to bed!" Ellen breathed, as the little boy wandered sleepily through the door, dressed in his yellow pajamas.

"No. Toby, you can't come with me," Ellen explained as

she felt the spell take a firmer hold. She was already feeling woozy, like she did when Mom gave her medicine. But Toby took no notice, he kept coming towards her and Ellen had no choice but to drop the cat and take Toby by the hand instead. She meant to take him back to bed, hoping against hope that the spell would last until she came back. But things did not work out that way. The spell had already gone too far, and the room began to spin and pieces of it seemed to peel away. The roaring, sucking, spinning noise grew louder. The darkness grew darker before it cleared, and the noises finally gave way to different noises—the babbling of voices and laughter.

Ellen was back on the roof. She still had the gold box clutched tightly in one hand. But she hadn't brought the witch cat back with her. Instead she had brought her little brother. Toby stood holding her hand tightly, and looking all around him with big round eyes.

Ellen bent down and put her arms round him.

"Oh, Toby, I'm sorry," she said. "I really didn't mean to."

10

The Halloween Revelries

"*G*ood Witching," sang a voice, and Ellen looked up to see Bobgoblin hopping towards them.

"Who's the yellow goblin?" he asked.

"He's not a goblin. He's my little brother!" said Ellen indignantly.

"He *looks* just like a goblin," said Bobgoblin and called some other goblins over to see.

"*Panslinging. Panslinging. Prepare for some panslinging,*" they cried, and before Ellen knew what was happening, the goblins had bundled Toby away and were showing him how to hop across rooftops and throw things about. Pots, pans, apple cores and half-eaten buns were flying everywhere. The goblins sang,

"Sling a bun
Mugs of grog
Roll like apple
Hop like frog,"

as they danced and played.

Toby, who was already quite good at throwing things, took part merrily.

"Yippeee!" cried the goblins.

"Yippeee!" cried Toby.

He was sliding all over the roof and the goblins were hopping about and making sure he did not fall over the edge. Then he went for a trip up in the sky and back, while Ellen watched and laughed at his laughter. He was having the time of his life.

Ellen decided to leave him for a while and go and look for Rufus. The roofs were now crowded with Halloween Revellers: witches, leaning on broomsticks and gossiping; wizards, amusing each other with little tricks; ghosts and monsters and fairies and beasts; everything she had ever dreamed of, in every shape and size. But Rufus was nowhere to be seen.

"Rufus, where are you?" Ellen called, hoping he might hear her.

"He's not coming to the Revelries," said a deep voice behind her. Ellen looked round and was delighted to see Extra Bright O'Glow towering into the sky.

"Rufus isn't coming?" she said. "But he must come. He wants to win his Medallion."

"He lost his uncle's Medallion and failed to return it. Weird Hannah won't let him attend the Revelries," said Extra Bright gloomily.

"But I've got the Medallion here," said Ellen. "We can return it to his uncle together. I'm going to get a wish."

"Then we must fetch him now," said Extra Bright. "The competitions are about to begin."

In spite of all the mischief Rufus had done, Ellen was feeling mean because she had not returned the Medallion earlier. She must help Rufus take the Medallion back to his uncle now, before it was too late.

At that moment, out of a crowd of gossiping witches, Weird Hannah appeared with a screech.

"There she is! The girl from the real world!" she cried.

"She stole my cloak! She wrecked my parlor! She broke my broomstick! She abducted my Rufus!"

"Ooh! I did not!" said Ellen indignantly. "It wasn't like that at all, and I only borrowed the cloak." By now everyone within earshot knew that she was from the real world, and a great surge of disapproval ran through the crowd. Real people, at the Revelries! It was practically unheard of. And what about the Haunters? The Haunters would get her if she was not careful. Weird Hannah did not much care for Ellen, but she was worrying herself to a shadow about her all the same. Ellen, however, had other things on her mind.

"Look what I've got," she said, holding out the box to show Weird Hannah. "I found it in the real world. It's Uncle Whizoon's Medallion. Now Rufus can come to the Revelries."

With a snort of disapproval, Weird Hannah took the box from Ellen and examined the Medallion. When she was sure it was really the one that she had polished two nights before, she put it back inside the box, and snapped the lid shut. She glared at Ellen, who said:

"Now Rufus can come to the Revelries and enter the spell competition." She looked hard at Hannah's crabby face, and added, "Please."

Weird Hannah hesitated for a moment, then she said,

"Well, all right. Fetch him quickly and tell him not to forget to change his socks."

Ellen and Extra Bright set off through the crowds. There was no time to lose. Ellen heard a loud voice above her head. An announcement was being made over a crackly loudspeaker.

"Will all competitors in the junior spell competition please take their places on the spell stand immediately."

"It's the witch children's spell competition," said Extra Bright. "It's about to start. We must find Rufus immediately or he'll be too late."

Ellen and Extra Bright moved on through the crowds saying, "Excuse me," and "Sorry," each time they trod on a toe, which was often, because Halloween creatures were milling about everywhere, and Extra Bright still had his boots on. He decided to take them off and leave them hanging on a television aerial until after the Revelries. It must have ruined someone's television picture below.

At last Ellen and Extra Bright found their way to Rufus's chimney. Ellen climbed into the pot and slid down inside. Extra Bright followed. He came down the chimney like water being poured from a jug. He formed a puddle of light in the parlor, then grew to be a tall glow again.

Rufus had gone to bed where he could sulk in peace. When he heard the loud thump as Ellen landed, he buried his face in the pillow.

"I've got it. I've got the Medallion!" said Ellen, picking herself up and running over to the bed.

"You're much too late," grumbled Rufus.

"No, I'm not," said Ellen. "If we find your uncle and return it quickly, there will still be time for you to enter the competition. Your mother says you can, but hurry." Rufus lifted his face from the pillow, but it was still as miserable as a week of wet Saturdays.

"Here's the Medallion," said Ellen and lifted the lid of the box to show Rufus. Like the sun coming from behind a cloud, Rufus's face lit up, slowly at first, and then, with a joyful whoop, he leapt out of bed.

"I know where my uncle will be!" he cried.

Extra Bright floated here and there and helped Rufus to get his things together, but it was a worse rush even than getting ready for Night Witchery classes. Ellen reminded Rufus to change his socks and he put on a beautiful black and gold stripy pair. Last of all he went to his mother's spell box and opened a large jar of silver powder. It twinkled so much that it could have been stardust. Rufus took a handful and pushed it well down into his pocket.

"Can't do spells without spell powder," he said, grinning.

Then, just as he was about to replace the top of the jar, he had an idea. He took a small handful of the powder and put it into Ellen's hand.

"What's that for?" asked Ellen in surprise.

"Just in case," said Rufus and he winked.

"Thank you!" said Ellen, excitedly, and she stuffed the powder into the back pocket of her jeans.

"Come along," said Extra Bright anxiously. "Time drifts on."

They returned immediately to the roof.

Still more Halloween Revellers were arriving out of the chimneys onto the roofs and the rooftops were beginning to look like a seaside promenade on a dark bank holiday. Many of the Revellers had already taken to the sky, which was a swirling sea of movement. Broom flyers, goblins, ghosts and fairies flitted and swept from tower block to tower block, from horizon to horizon. The largest full moon that Ellen had ever seen hung in the middle of it all, with wisps of cloud around it like an old man's beard.

"I know where the wizards will be," said Rufus, pulling Ellen behind him through the crowd. Extra Bright, wonderfully graceful without his boots, glided along behind them. As they rushed up and over the house roofs and then across the warehouse, they were joined by a crowd of goblins and Toby.

"We're off to see the wizards. We wish to see Uncle Whizoon," sang the goblins in a tune that Ellen thought she had heard somewhere before.

The chattering, singing, scurrying group raced along the next row of houses and across some garages, until they arrived at a wide stretch of rooftops where several platforms, like small football stands, had been set up. They were lit up with neon lights that winked on and off, and were filled with rows of wizards.

"That's Uncle Whizoon over there," said Rufus, pointing to a particularly fine-looking wizard in the front row. He had more moons and stars on his hat than anyone else.

When Uncle Whizoon saw Rufus and Ellen and Extra Bright O'Glow, Toby and the goblins all waving and shouting at him, he stood up. He leaned over the front of the stand to speak to them.

"Ah, Rufus," said Uncle Whizoon. "Welcome." Then he looked at Ellen, who was out of breath but grinning from ear to ear. "This must be your friend from the real world. She is brave to venture thus far abroad at night, and more so on Halloween. You have brought with you the Medallion?"

"Yes. It's here," panted Rufus. "Ellen has it. She asks, in return, a wish."

"Very well," said the wizard. "Child from the real world, your bravery shall be rewarded. One seldom sees a child so faithful and so true." He smiled a stately smile and some of his neighboring wizards clapped like spectators at a cricket match.

Now, in fact, Ellen had not realized how brave it was to venture onto the rooftops at Halloween, and she was beginning to feel embarrassed about the praise she did not deserve. But she had come here for a wish, so she had better get on with it. She opened the gold box which she still had in her hand. Rufus took out the Medallion, and held it out to the old wizard, and Ellen opened her mouth to make a wish. But before she could speak, a great black shadow swooped down low over the stand and everybody ducked.

The wizards, the goblins, the ghosts, Ellen, Rufus, everyone looked up into the sky. Flying among the wispy clouds was what looked like a flock of enormous birds. They were the size of small airplanes, had huge strong wings and sharp talons and they were circling like hungry vultures.

There was a loud intake of breath as the whole crowd gasped.

"It's the Halloween Haunters!" cried Rufus. "They're after Ellen!"

"Hide her. Hide her. Hide Ellen from the Haunters!" cried the goblins, scurrying around in confusion. Toby broke away from the goblins and ran to hold Ellen's hand.

"What tiresome creatures they are," said Uncle Whizoon wearily. "Rufus, hang the Medallion around my neck. With my power restored I can grant the child safe conduct back to the real world."

Rufus climbed onto the stand and the wizard removed his hat so that the witch boy could put the chain of the Medallion over his head and around his neck.

But a gigantic Hideous Haunter was already swooping low again and, before anyone could say anything (even Uncle Whizoon, who was very stately but very slow) the Haunter had snatched Ellen up in his talons, and whisked her off the roof. Toby was still holding on to Ellen's hand very tightly, and both children were swept, with a chilling cry of delight from the Haunter, into the sky. They looked like the tail of a monstrous kite.

"Children from the real world are not allowed at the Revelries!" howled the Haunter.

All Ellen could see, when she looked up, was that a huge scaly foot had hold of the back of her sweater and was pulling her and Toby up towards the clouds. Higher and higher they went, until they had left all the other Halloween Revellers far behind. The lights of the town spread for miles beneath them.

"I only came for a wish," whispered Ellen, and the Haunter laughed a horrible laugh.

"You wish to meddle in the land of Dreams?" he cried. "Now you shall see the land of Nightmares!" And his howls of laughter were as loud as claps of thunder when it crashes over your house in the middle of the night.

Toby could not see the danger. He was enjoying the ride. As they sped higher and faster up through the blanket of thickening cloud, Ellen found to her horror that Toby's small hand was slipping out of hers.

"Oh, no, Toby!" she cried, as Toby started falling away from her, down, down, down and back through the cloud. Ellen was dragged ever upwards towards the stars and soon she could no longer see him. This Halloween was turning into the worst night of her life.

II

The Land
of Nightmares

*B*ut Toby was having the best night of his life. This was the most exciting thing that had happened to him since he had accidentally come down the school slide backwards. He was quietly singing to himself, "Wheeee, wheee!" as he went around and around, down and down.

He passed a helicopter, at a distance, and then there was a loud cheer from below as he appeared from out of the clouds. He fell past an owl who was very surprised to see him, then a whole cluster of moths. There was certainly plenty to look at up here in the sky.

Meanwhile, the goblins were running hither and thither to prepare a soft landing for him. As he hurtled down to the rooftops, they caught him in a large bedspread, held by four goblins, one at each corner. Toby bounced several times before he came to rest and lay on the blanket laughing merrily.

The goblins lifted him out of the blanket and placed him on his feet. They gave him a mug of cocoa and generally fussed about him and busied themselves with the task of explaining why he could not be dropped from the sky again.

Then they danced and sang,

"Children dropping from the sky
Will reach the rooftops by and by
Find a blanket, hold it high,
For babes can't fly, don't ask us why."

Now the Revelries were really in full swing and everyone was having a marvellous time. That is, everyone but Rufus, who was sitting on a gable, clutching his knees, and gazing up into the sky. He had watched Ellen disappear into the clouds in the clutches of the Hideous Haunter, and, although others who had been watching were muttering, "People from the real world are not allowed at the Revelries, anyway," and

"Serves her right," and so on, he felt very bad about the way things had turned out. After all, the land of Nightmares was a terrible place to be at the best of times, but particularly at Halloween.

Now it was time for him to take part in the spell contest. This was when he was going to prove that, when it came to spell casting, he was better than anyone. He was going to win his own Medallion and be admitted to the Grand Order of Middle Magic. He had been waiting for this moment ever since he had cast his first spell on his teddy bear when he was only three years old.

His name had already been announced twice over the loud-speaker as the next contestant, and the announcer was becoming tired of waiting for him.

"*The next contestant,*" crackled the voice, "*is Rufus, son of Weird Hannah Chimney-Witch. Will Rufus Chimney-Witch please come to the stand to perform his prepared spell. This is the final announcement.*"

Rufus looked first at Weird Hannah, who was waving her broomstick about on a roof nearby and screaming at him to get himself to the stand immediately, before it was too late, or she'd turn him into a frog. Then he looked at Uncle Whizoon, who had returned to the wizard stand and was talking wisely with other wizards. He saw that the goblins were busy playing with Toby, and that Extra Bright O'Glow was hovering above him and muttering anxiously, "Poor little lass, I warned her about the Halloween Haunters."

Rufus had never felt very heroic, but there was something about this year's Halloween Revelries that made him feel different. He jumped to his feet and sent a tile crashing down the gable and into a gutter. He had made up his mind. He grabbed a nearby broomstick that no one seemed to be using. He climbed aboard and shot off the rooftop like a missile in search of a target. He had no idea what he was going to do when he got there, but he was going to the land of Nightmares. If Ellen was going to be stuck there for the rest of Halloween, then he was going to be there by her side.

As Rufus came up through the cloud, it was like a submarine-launched rocket zipping out of the water. Now, all around him the starry sky stretched on for ever. He could just see Ellen, a tiny struggling figure, being dragged by the horrible monster into one end of a tunnel. It was the tunnel through the sky that led to the land of Nightmares.

The Hideous Haunter's howls of laughter were echoing around and around the tunnel, and to Ellen they were deafening. She had been struggling from time to time to free herself, but it was no use. The Hideous Haunter just gripped her sweater more tightly. Ellen was having to use her hands to brush off clammy sticky things and spiky-legged spidery things that were trying to cling to her face and were getting tangled in her hair. She had never minded creepy crawly things at home. In fact, she was rather fond of spiders. But these were sticking to her face and eyelashes, and she was wildly waving her arms about and kicking her feet. The Haunter was pulling her relentlessly on, and she stopped kicking to rest for a moment. Then she called to him, "This is certainly a good place to make nightmares!"

"Oh, this is just the beginning," answered the Haunter. "It gets much better as you go on."

Ellen said nothing. She had started untwining a daddy-long-legs from her hair.

"You're lucky," the Haunter roared. "Most people from the real world don't get a chance to try our nightmares."

"I see," said Ellen distractedly. She flicked the daddy-long-legs back down the tunnel and it flew away.

I wish I could fly away, she thought miserably. Nightmares are bad enough when you are asleep, but they're even worse when you're awake because you can't wake up to be rid of them.

Ellen did not want to go any further with the Hideous Haunter. She had only one faint hope of escape. She still had the magic powder that Rufus had given her in her back jeans pocket and now it was crackling fiercely. She also knew that in order to make the spell she needed a rhyme to go with the magic powder. As she was swept through the tunnel, she desperately tried to remember some of the poems she had written in school. There were many, and they were good. But she couldn't think of any of them now. She tried to remember some famous poems she had learned.

"I wandered lonely as a cloud . . ." she whispered to herself, and put her hand over the powder in her pocket. She did not want to waste it by using it with the wrong rhyme. She knocked a moth off her nose.

"When I was three, I was hardly me . . ." she tried. Then, as she brushed past a spider on his web, she tried, *"Little Miss Muffet sat on a tuffet . . ."*

But none of these seemed right, and now they were at the end of the tunnel. They had arrived in the land of Nightmares, where it was a dark, misty night.

Ellen felt solid ground beneath her feet again as the Haunter dropped her onto something that felt like concrete. She fell and grazed her knees, but she said nothing. She didn't want to break the eerie silence. There were two pale streetlights that threw strange shadows, and tall unlit buildings all around. The Haunter guided Ellen towards a big, black warehouse.

The door of the warehouse creaked open and, although it was only dimly lit, Ellen caught a glimpse of what was inside. The warehouse was full of sighing shadows and Hideous Haunters playing cards.

Ellen's Haunter bundled her into the warehouse and closed the door, which whined and clicked shut. The Haunters inside looked up gloomily, and then returned to their silent game of cards. They all had talons, huge black wings folded over their backs, and yellow, slitty eyes.

A Haunter sat at a desk near the door and marked Ellen's name off on a list as she went past. That felt like arriving late at school and having an 'L' put by your name on the class register. Ellen shuddered. It was so cold and dismal in here. The Haunters did not seem to be enjoying their game of cards either.

The Haunter at the desk said in a hoarse, scratchy voice, "Show her some nightmares. She can start at Number One. When you get to One Hundred, give her a cup of tea."

"I don't like tea," whispered Ellen. But no one heard.

Ellen's Haunter nodded. Even he was not laughing in here. This place was no laughing matter.

"She can choose a nightmare and take it home as a souvenir," said the Haunter at the desk.

"I don't want a nightmare as a souvenir," whispered Ellen. No one heard.

Ellen was led across the hall into a room with *Nightmare Number One* scrawled across the door in chalk. Underneath it said, *Haunters Rule O.K?* Ellen's Haunter opened the door and gently eased her inside.

The door shut behind her. The room was brightly lit and made Ellen's eyes hurt, but when she got used to the light, she saw a table piled high with her favorite food—candy, cakes, pastries, spaghetti rings, hamburgers without pickles, french fries, all smelling delicious. What sort of a nightmare was this? she wondered. Ellen went towards the table, but when she reached out to touch the food, it gave way.

It was all made of gelatin. And she fell forwards into it, but now it wasn't gelatin at all, it was oatmeal! She was in a lake of the horrible stuff. She was trying to move, and was not getting anywhere, but she knew that she must get to the other side somehow. With a heavy sick feeling, she decided that if worse came to worst, she would have to eat herself out. But first she would try to swim. She made one last, almighty effort with her arms, and just managed to move them around in a sort of breast stroke. Then she pushed with her legs at the same time, and forced her head through the gungy mess. Then again her arms, then her legs. Now she was moving, slowly, but she was moving. Finally, worn out, but relieved, she fell out of the lake onto dry land. She looked down at herself. She was covered in oatmeal but safe.

She saw a door, ran to it and opened it. She stepped through and found herself in a passage. For a moment she thought that she could run to safety, but her heart sank when she blinked her eyes to get used to the gloom and saw her Hideous Haunter standing like a shadow and waiting for her.

"Well? What did you think of that one?" he asked.

"Not much," said Ellen.

It was just at that moment that Rufus had slipped through the warehouse door. Now he had to get past the desk at the entrance. The Hideous Haunters all looked up from their game again. The one at the desk asked Rufus for his name. When he couldn't find it on his list, he was going to kick him back down the tunnel to the sky, but Rufus distracted him by saying that he could see one of the other Haunters breaking a Hideous Haunter rule. He was smiling during a card game! The Haunter at the desk kicked the smiling Haunter back down the tunnel instead. Meanwhile, Rufus ran across the hall of the warehouse, into Nightmare Number One. The other Haunters turned back to their cards.

Ellen and her Haunter were on their way to Nightmare Number Two. Ellen was still running through possible spell rhymes in her head and had now reached *"We all live in a yellow submarine. . . ."*

She was going to have to try something no matter how wrong it sounded. She had no intention of going through any more nightmares. Cold oatmeal was bad enough, but next she might find herself swimming through a lake of carrot soup!

They arrived at the door with *Nightmare Number Two* scrawled on it, just as Rufus came out of the back door of Nightmare Number One. He looked a terrible sight. He was covered in cobwebs and oatmeal. He was staggering along the passage towards Ellen.

"Ellen, Ellen!" he cried. "Have you still got the powder?"

Ellen swung around in delight, her heart leaping like a flea on a sheet. The Hideous Haunter growled and grabbed hold of her arm.

"Yes! Yes! I've got the powder here!" said Ellen, and she wriggled a bit as she took the powder from her back pocket with the other hand.

Rufus, in a great burst of heroism, suddenly remembered everything that he had been taught at Night Witchery classes, and he came up with an excellent rhyme for a spell.

"Dreamer say! Dreamer say!
Hideous Haunter drop your prey!
Fly away! Fly into day!
Dreamer, dreamer, do not stay!"

The Haunter and Ellen were still in the doorway of Nightmare Number Two, when Ellen started shrieking out each line of the verse that Rufus called out. She scattered the magic powder all over the Haunter's feet and hands. It sparkled in the gloom, like stardust. The Haunter was confused. Ellen kept shouting and scattering. The door to the nightmare snapped shut on the Haunter's toe, and he howled. The spell began.

It was not a big one. Nothing spectacular. After all, it was Ellen's first. But it worked. It worked well enough to cause a sort of itch in the hand by which the Haunter was holding

Ellen. The itch, the confusion, the shouting, the door closing on his toe, were all enough to make the Haunter loosen his grip on Ellen, just for a second.

Ellen pulled her arm away and ran helter-skelter like a surprised crab down the passage. Rufus took her hand and they ran together through Nightmare Number One. They helped each other through the oatmeal and finally fell out of the front door and into the hall, where the silent card game went endlessly on. They were just dodging, hand in hand, between the tables, when the alarm bell rang. It was like a hundred telephones all ringing together. As one, the Haunters rose from their chairs and Ellen and Rufus made for the door as fast as the oatmeal on their feet would allow.

But they were too late. Before they reached the door, the Haunter from the desk had lifted himself from his chair and slammed and bolted it. Ellen and Rufus slid to a halt, changed direction and ran into the shadows. There they crouched like two mice in a cattery.

The Haunters were knocking over tables and chairs to look underneath for Rufus and Ellen. Their cards scattered everywhere. Some Haunters had enormous cudgels in their hands and they were poking them into shadowy corners. One Haunter even had a long stick with a spiky ball on a chain at the end. The spiky ball looked like a giant gooseberry, and, much to the annoyance of the other Haunters, he kept swinging it around his head and shouting.

Eventually Ellen and Rufus had to leave the shadows or be squashed by a cudgel. They rushed out into the hall and made for the door again, hoping to break it open. The Haunter with the spiky ball followed them, shouting. He swung at them, but the iron ball missed Ellen and Rufus and crashed, instead, through the wooden door, with a loud splintering sound. They jumped without delay through the hole it had made, and ran under the dim streetlights across the dark concrete to the tunnel that led to the sky.

Although they were graceful in the air, the Haunters were clumsy on the ground, and they couldn't move fast enough to prevent Ellen and Rufus from hurling themselves into the tunnel and bumping and rolling down through the creepy-crawlies and the blackness, down, down, down until they fell higgledy-piggledy into the open sky.

Morning was not far away and the Haunters hated day-light, so a crowd of them gathered to watch Ellen and Rufus disappear down the tunnel. They did not follow. They lashed their tails and roared. Ellen's Haunter blew his nose hard on a big handkerchief. He did not want the other Haunters to know how upset he was. But life up there in the land of Nightmares was very boring without visitors, and he had never yet been able to make one stay. He sniffed and sighed and reflected on how very unfair life could be.

12
The End

*A*s Ellen and Rufus fell through the sky, the rushing night air cleared the spiders and moths and oatmeal from their hair, but Ellen still had butterflies in her stomach. She and Rufus were high enough to be able to see that the sun was about to come up.

While they were falling, first close together, then further apart, then closer together again, Ellen had time to worry about where and how they were going to land. As Rufus came close, she told him that she didn't want to splash down in the pond as she had done quite enough swimming for one day, and neither did she want to be found in the morning, hanging by her sweater from the church steeple.

Rufus grinned and winked and did a somersault. He still had his spell powder and tonight he was a hero and nothing could stop him. He decided to do the spell that he had been going to do in the spell competition, had it started to rain. Out of thin air, as he fell down and around like a sky-diver, he magicked an enormous black umbrella! It was just like the one that Ellen's father took with him to work when it looked like rain. It even had a button that you pressed to make it fly open. Rufus pressed the button, and with a rushing sound the umbrella opened just like a parachute. Next time Ellen came close enough to Rufus, she too grabbed the handle, and they sailed gently Earthwards.

They drifted through the clouds, down towards apartment buildings and factories, the park, Ellen's road with the warehouses behind it, and the rooftops where they had begun. They made a perfect landing on the roof where, by now, there were only a few Revellers left to welcome them.

The Revelries were nearly over. The competitions had finished and the Revellers were drifting back to their chimneys.

"By the way, did you win your Medallion?" Ellen asked Rufus, as he carefully collapsed his new umbrella.

"Maybe next year," said Rufus shrugging.

He was, in fact, very disappointed that he had missed the competition, but it was too late now, so he decided not to say so.

Weird Hannah was making her way towards them and Uncle Whizoon was the only wizard left in the wizard stand. All the others had got tired and gone home. Weird Hannah arrived and asked Rufus where on earth he had been all this time, said that the umbrella might come in useful one day, she supposed, and that Rufus would worry her to a shadow. Uncle Whizoon, in the stand, smiled a stately smile. Then his taxi-stick arrived to take him home. After a long hunt for his wand, which he had mislaid while talking to the other wizards, he made his way down from the stand.

"You see, Rufus," he said, when at last he was down the steps, "the courage of the child from the real world has made you brave."

Ellen was becoming embarrassed again. The wizard walked slowly up to Rufus who was thinking that bravery was all very well—but perhaps, after all, he would rather have had a Medallion. The witch boy tried to smile, but it wasn't very successful. Then, to Rufus's utter amazement, Uncle Whizoon took his own Medallion from around his neck and put it over Rufus's head.

"Take my Medallion," said the old wizard. "Tonight you have earned it. Your umbrella spell could prove to be one of the most popular in the country. I shall have another one made."

The Medallion lay glowing on Rufus's chest and his face glowed as brightly with pride. So he had won the Medallion of Middle Magic after all!

"I told you I could do spells," said Rufus to Ellen, and he ran off to find a glass window-pane that he could use as a mirror to admire himself.

"And now you, child," said Uncle Whizoon, turning to Ellen. "What is your wish? Make haste, for the night is nearly over."

Although Ellen had made up her mind to wish that Richard would fail his exam and stay at home with her and the rest of the family, that idea now seemed to come from a very long time ago. She knew now, with everyone being so brave and successful, that that sort of wish just would not be right.

She felt a bit cheated, but all the same, she smiled sweetly and said:

"I wish that my brother, Richard, would pass his music exam, and stay with Grandma if he wants to, even though I don't want him to go."

And that was that. The wish was made. The deed was done. She felt much better.

"Then your wish shall be granted," said Uncle Whizoon. "And now, child, you must return to the real world. This rooftop is no place for you, and my taxi-stick awaits."

"Thank you," said Ellen.

She said a brief but warm farewell to the goblins and Extra Bright O'Glow and Weird Hannah, but Rufus was nowhere to be found. He was polishing his Medallion behind a chimney somewhere and practicing a spell on a beetle.

"Say goodbye to Rufus for me," said Ellen to the goblins. "Say thank you for everything."

"*We will, we will. We wish you well,*" sang the goblins. "*Let wizard wise unwind the spell.*"

Ellen put her arms around Toby who was asleep over a chimney pot. She gave him a hug and held him firmly.

"By the way, who's doing the spell?" she asked.

So the goblins rushed off to call Uncle Whizoon back. He

was just climbing onto his taxi-stick because he had forgotten all about sending Ellen home.

"Ah, the spell," said Uncle Whizoon.

Very hurriedly, because his taxi was waiting, he said,

"Till night owls, fears and bats have fled
Be safe and snug and warm in bed."

Then he waved his wand about and, with a tinkling of bells, puffs of smoke, showers of sparks and many other wonderful things, Ellen found herself back in her own bedroom.

She was standing by the window, and morning was already creeping across the sky. As she looked back into her room she realized that Toby was asleep in her bed.

"Will they never get the spell right?" she muttered and she took Toby back to his own bed and tucked him in. He hardly woke. Just sighed the deepest of sighs, ground his teeth a little, and sank back into the deepest of sleeps.

Ellen hurried back to her own room. There was so little of the night left. But once she had dropped off she must have slept deeply too, because, when she woke an hour or two later, she felt very good indeed.

Ellen got up, got dressed, did her hair and danced down for breakfast, taking the last four stairs in one leap. She was all ready for school.

"Good morning, dear," Mom greeted her. "You look much better today. Every time I looked in on you yesterday, you were asleep."

"Yes. We were worried about you," said Dad. "Are you sure you're all right?"

"Quite sure," said Ellen.

Then Toby got into trouble for throwing a piece of crust across the room. Ellen picked it up and put it back on his plate and Toby beamed at her lovingly. Ellen sat down next to Richard, who was looking unusually sullen and downcast.

"Don't worry, Richard," said Ellen. "I'm sorry about last night, and you're going to pass your exam. I know you are." And she tried to wink. Richard looked at her oddly. Then he brightened up, because suddenly, for no reason he could think of, he knew that it was true.

Ellen started her breakfast.

She was just finishing her Rice Krispies, when the kitchen door opened, very slightly, and, to everyone's surprise, in walked an enormous black cat. Ellen, who should not have been, was the most surprised of all. She reached down and stroked the cat, who rubbed around her legs and purred like a pneumatic drill.

"Good gracious!" said Mom. "Wherever did that cat come from? Whoever does it belong to?"

"I don't think it belongs to anyone around here," said Ellen, innocently. "Perhaps we should keep it."

And, since the family never did find out where the cat had come from, that's what they did.